Phonics Friends

Lilly's Lost Lunch
The Sound of **L**

The
**Child's
World**

By Joanne Meier and Cecilia Minden

The Child's World

Published in the United States of America
by The Child's World®
PO Box 326
Chanhassen, MN 55317-0326
800-599-READ
www.childsworld.com

A special thank you to the Ascencio family for providing
the location and modeling for this book and the Courtney
family for allowing "Misty" to debut.

The Child's World®: Mary Berendes, Publishing Director

Editorial Directions, Inc.: E. Russell Primm, Editorial
Director and Project Editor; Katie Marsico, Associate
Editor; Judith Shiffer, Associate Editor and School Media
Specialist; Linda S. Koutris, Photo Researcher and
Selector

The Design Lab: Kathleen Petelinsek, Design and Page
Production

Photographs ©: Photo setting and photography by Romie
and Alice Flanagan/Flanagan Publishing Services: cover,
6, 8, 10, 12, 14, 16, 18, 20; Corbis: 4.

Library of Congress Cataloging-in-Publication Data
Meier, Joanne.
  Lilly's lost lunch : the sound of L / by Joanne Meier and
Cecilia Minden.
    p. cm. — (Phonics friends)
  Summary: Lilly misplaces her lunch while getting ready
for school, in simple text featuring the "l" sound.
  ISBN 1-59296-299-8 (library bound : alk. paper) [1.
English language—Phonetics. 2. Reading.] I. Meier,
Joanne D. II. Title. III. Series.
  PZ7.6539Li 2004
  [E]—dc22   2004002200

Note to parents and educators:
The Child's World® has created Phonics Friends with the goal of exposing children to engaging stories and pictures that assist in phonics development. The books in the series will help children learn the relationships between the letters of written language and the individual sounds of spoken language. This contact helps children learn to use these relationships to read and write words.

The books in this series follow a similar format. An introductory page, to be read by an adult, introduces the child to the phonics feature, or sound, that will be highlighted in the book. Read this page to the child, stressing the phonic feature. Help the student learn how to form the sound with her mouth. The Phonics Friends story and engaging photographs follow the introduction. At the end of the story, word lists categorize the feature words into their phonic element. Additional information on using these lists is on The Child's World® Web site listed at the top of this page.

Each book in this series has been carefully written to meet specific readability requirements. Close attention has been paid to elements such as word count, sentence length, and vocabulary. Readability formulas measure the ease with which the text can be read and understood. Each Phonics Friends book has been analyzed using the Spache readability formula. For more information on this formula, as well as the levels for each of the books in this series please visit The Child's World® Web site.

Reading research suggests that systematic phonics instruction can greatly improve students' word recognition, spelling, and comprehension skills. The Phonics Friends series assists in the teaching of phonics by providing students with important opportunities to apply their knowledge of phonics as they read words, sentences, and text.

This is the letter *l*.

In this book, you will read words that have the *l* sound as in:

late, left, lost, and *lunch.*

It is a busy morning

at Lilly's house.

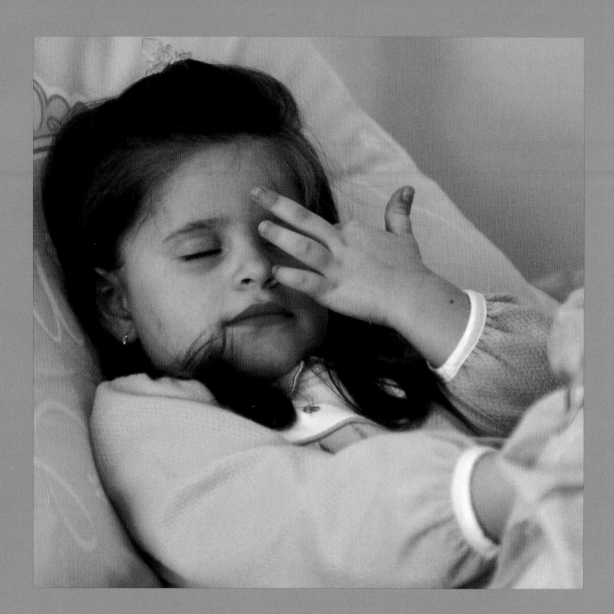

Lilly wakes up late.

She does not like to get up.

Her left shoe is lost.

She has to look a long time.

"Lilly, time for breakfast!
It's getting cold. Let's go!"
said Dad.

Lilly doesn't listen. She likes to play with her dog Lucky.

"Lilly, let's go! We will be late for school."

Oh no! Lilly's lunch is lost.

Where could it be?

Lilly and her dad look and look.

"Where did you see it last?"

asks Dad.

It was on the little table.

Oh look! Lucky likes lunch, too.

Fun Facts

It is easy to hear a door slam or a bell ring, but it is harder to listen to other noises. When a doctor wants to listen to your heart or lungs, she needs to use a special instrument called a stethoscope. Some people don't like listening to loud noises or might have a hard time falling asleep if there is noise around them. These people often buy earplugs so they don't have to listen to sounds they don't want to hear.

You have probably heard that breakfast is the most important meal of the day, but you need to eat lunch and dinner, too! In 2003, the president proclaimed one week each year to be National School Lunch Week. During this week, which always begins on the second Sunday in October, kids have a chance to learn about nutrition and eating healthily.

Activity

Planning a Healthy Lunch for Your Friends

National School Lunch Week is in October, but you should practice healthy eating habits every day. Talk to your parents about inviting your friends to a party at your house where only healthy foods will be served for lunch. Instead of chips, offer vegetables. For a main course, consider making sandwiches with whole wheat bread and a lean meat such as turkey. You can serve yogurt and fresh fruit for dessert.

To Learn More

Books
About the Sound of L
Flanagan, Alice. *Left: The Sound of L.* Chanhassen, Minn.: The Child's World, 2000.

About Listening
Graham, Terry Lynne. *Listening Is a Way of Loving.* Atlanta: Humanics Learning, 1994.
King, Mary Ellen. *A Good Day for Listening.* Ridgefield, Conn.: Morehouse Publishing, 1995.
Meiners, Chris J. *Listen and Learn.* Minneapolis: Free Spirit Publishing, 2003.

About Lunch
Ehlert, Louise. *Feathers for Lunch.* San Diego: Harcourt Brace Jovanovich, 1990.
Nagel, Karen Berman, and Jerry Zimmerman (illustrator). *The Lunch Line.* New York: Scholastic, 1996.
Palatini, Margie, and Howard Fine (illustrator). *Zak's Lunch.* New York: Clarion Books, 1998.

Web Sites
Visit our home page for lots of links about the Sound of L:
http://www.childsworld.com/links.html

Note to Parents, Teachers, and Librarians: We routinely check our Web links to make sure they're safe, active sites—so encourage your readers to check them out!

L Feature Words

Proper names
Lilly
Lucky

**Feature Words in
Initial Position**
last
late
left
let's
like
listen
little
long
look
lost
lunch

About the Authors

Joanne Meier, PhD, has worked as an elementary school teacher and university professor. She earned her BA in early childhood education from the University of South Carolina, and her MEd and PhD in education from the University of Virginia. She currently works as a literacy consultant for schools and private organizations. Joanne Meier lives with her husband Eric, and spends most of her time chasing her two daughters, Kella and Erin, and her two cats, Sam and Gilly, in Charlottesville, Virginia.

Cecilia Minden, PhD, directs the Language and Literacy Program at the Harvard Graduate School of Education. She is a reading specialist with classroom and administrative experience in grades K–12. She earned her PhD in reading education from the University of Virginia. Cecilia and her husband Dave Cupp enjoy sharing their love of reading with their granddaughter Chelsea.